The Magic Lamp and Other Santal Folk-Tales

The Magic Lamp and Other Santal Folk-Tales

A. Campbell

Hawk Press

Published by

Hawk Press
4836/24, Ansari Road, Daryaganj
New Delhi – 110 002
Phones : 9643330713, +91-11-23278618, +91-11-35676207
E-mail: thehawkpress@gmail.com
www.thehawkpress.com

Contents

Preface

Of late years the Folk tales of India have been the subject of much study and research, and several interesting collections of them have been published. But I am not aware that the folk lore of the Santals, has received the attention which it deserved. The Santals as a people, have, to a remarkable degree, succeeded in resisting the subtle Hinduising influences to which they have long been exposed, and to which such a large number of aboriginal tribes have succumbed. Retaining their language in institutions, tribal organization, and religion almost intact. Their traditions show the jealousy with which these have been guarded, and the suspicion and distrust with which contact with their Aryan neighbours was regarded. The point at which they have been most accessible to outward influence and example, is in their relations with the aboriginal tribes, who in a more or less degree have merged themselves in Hinduism. Hindu ideas, customs and beliefs, filtering through these tribes, became considerably modified before they reached the Santals, and were therefore less potent in their effects than if they had been drawn from the fountain head of Hinduism itself. Still, in respect to their aboriginal neighbours they are always on their guard, ready to repel any innovation on their customs or religion with which they may be threatened. In the folk tales of such a people we may well expect to find something, if not altogether new, still interesting and instructive from an ethnological point of view, and this expectation, I believe, would be abundantly gratified if they were only made accessible to those who, by training and study, are competent to deal with them.

Santal folk-tales may be divided into two classes—those apparently purely Santal in their origin, and those obtained from other sources. Those of the first class are by far the more numerous, and besides showing the superstitious awe [ii]with which the Santals regard the creations of their own fancy, they throw a flood of light upon the social customs and usages of this most interesting people. The second class embraces a large number of the more popular tales current among the Hindus and semi-Hinduised aborigines. These, although adapted and modified by the Santals to suit their language, modes of thought, and social usages, may generally be detected by the presence of proper names, or untranslatable phrases which unmistakably indicate the source from which they have been derived.

These tales were taken down in Santali at first hand, and are therefore genuine and redolent of the soil. In translating them the author himself allowed considerable latitude without in any way diverging so far from the original as to in any degree impair their value to the student of Indian Folk-lore.

It was to be expected that in the popular tales of a simple, unpolished people like the Santals, expressions and allusions unfitted for ears polite would be found. In all such cases the changes which have been made are in accord with Santal thought and usage, so that the tales are, notwithstanding these alterations, thoroughly Santali.

I have aimed at making these Santal Folk-tales, in their English dress, true to the forests and hills of their nativity. I am not without hope, that in this I have succeeded in some small degree.

A number of the tales included in this volume have already appeared in the Indian Evangelical Review, but in this collected form they are more likely to prove of service to those who take an interest in the subject.

This volume of Santal Folk-Tales is offered as a humble contribution to the Folk-lore of India.

The Magic Lamp

In the capital of a certain raja, there lived a poor widow. She had an only son who was of comely form and handsome countenance. One day a merchant from a far country came to her house, and standing in front of the door called out, "dada, dada," (elder brother). The widow replied, "He is no more, he died many years ago." On hearing this the merchant wept bitterly, mourning the loss of his younger brother. He remained some days in his sister-in-law's house, at the end of which he said to her, "This lad and I will go in quest of the golden flowers, prepare food for our journey." Early next morning they set out taking provisions with them for the way. After they had gone a considerable distance, the boy being fatigued said, "Oh! uncle I can go no further." The merchant scolded him, and walked along as fast as he could. After some time the boy again said, "I am so tired I can go no further." His uncle turned back and beat him, and he, nerved by fear, walked rapidly along the road. At length they reached a hill, to the summit of which they climbed, and gathered a large pile of firewood. They had no fire with them, but the merchant ordered his nephew to blow with his mouth as if he were kindling the embers of a fire. He blew until he was exhausted, and then said, "What use is there in blowing when there is no fire?" The merchant replied "Blow, or I shall beat you." He again blew with all his might for a short time, and then stopping, said, "There is no fire, how can it possibly burn?" on which the merchant struck him. The lad then redoubled his efforts, and presently the pile of firewood burst into a blaze. On the firewood being consumed, an iron trap-door appeared underneath the ashes, and the merchant ordered his nephew to pull it up. He pulled, but finding himself unable to open it, said, "It will not open." The merchant told him to pull with greater force, and he, being afraid lest he should be again beaten, pulled with all his might, but could not raise it. He again said, "It will not open," whereupon the merchant struck him, and ordered him to try again. Applying himself with all his might, he at length succeeded. On the door being raised, they saw a lamp burning, and beside it an immense quantity of golden flowers.

The merchant then said to the boy, "As you enter do not touch any of the gold flowers, but put out the lamp, and heap on the gold tray as many of the gold flowers as you can, and bring them away with you." He did as he was ordered, and on reaching the door again requested his uncle to relieve him of the gold flowers, but he refused, saying, "Climb up as best as you can." The boy replied, "How can I do so, when my hands are full?" The merchant then shut the iron trap door on him, and went away to a distant country.

The boy being imprisoned in the dark vault, wept bitterly, and having no food, in a few days he became very weak. Taking the lamp in his hand, he sat down in a corner, and without knowing what he was doing, began to rub the lamp with his hand. A ring, which he wore on his finger, came into contact with the lamp, and immediately a fairy issued from it, and asked, "What is it you want with me?" He replied, "Open the door and let me out." The fairy opened the door, and the boy went home taking the lamp with him. Being hungry, he asked for food, but his mother replied, "There is nothing in the house that I can give you." He then went for his lamp, saying, "I will clean it, and then sell it, and with the money buy food." Taking the lamp in his hand he began to rub it, and his ring again touching it, a fairy issued from it and said "What do you wish for?" The boy said "Cooked rice and uncooked rice." The fairy immediately brought him an immense quantity of both kinds of rice.

Sometime after this, certain merchants brought horses for sale, and the boy seeing them wished to buy one. Having no money, he remembered his lamp, and taking it up, pressed his ring against it, and the fairy instantly appeared, and asked him what he wanted. He said, "Bring me a horse," and immediately the fairy presented to him an immense number of horses.

When the boy had become a young man, it so happened, that one day the raja's daughter was being carried to the ghat to bathe, and he seeing her palki with the attendants passing, went to his mother and said, "I am going to see the princess." She tried to dissuade him, but he insisted on her giving him permission, so at length she gave him leave. He went secretly, and saw her as she was bathing, and on returning home, said to his mother, "I have seen the princess, and I am in love with her. Go, and inform the raja that your son loves his daughter, and begs her hand in marriage." His mother said, "Do you think the raja will consider us as on an equality with him?" He would not, however, be gainsaid, but kept urging her daily to carry his message to the raja, until she being wearied with his importunity went to the palace, and being admitted to an audience, informed the raja that her son was enamoured of the princess, his daughter, and begged that she might be given to him in marriage. The raja made answer that on her son giving him a large sum of money which he named, and which would have been beyond the means of the raja himself, he would be prepared to give his daughter in marriage to her son. The young man had recourse to his lamp and ring, and the fairy supplied him with a much larger sum of money than the raja had demanded. He took it all, and gave it to the raja, who was astonished beyond measure at the sight of such immense wealth.

After a reasonable time the old mother was sent to the raja to request him to fulfil his promise, but he, being reluctant to see his daughter united to one so much her inferior in station, in hope of being relieved from the obligation to fulfil his promise, demanded that a palace suited to her rank and station in life be prepared for her, after which he would no longer delay the nuptials. The would-be bridegroom applied to his never failing friends, his lamp and ring, and on the fairy appearing begged him to build a large castle in one night, and to furnish and adorn it as befitted the residence of a raja's daughter. The fairy complied with the request, and the whole city was amazed next morning at the sight of a lordly castle, where the evening before there had not been even a hut. The dewan tried to dissuade the raja, but without effect, and in due time the marriage was celebrated amid great rejoicings.

On a certain day, some time after the marriage, the raja and his son-in-law went to the forest to hunt. During their absence, the merchant to whom reference has already been made, arrived at the castle gate, bearing in his hand a new lamp which he offered in exchange to the princess for any old lamp she might possess. She thought it a good opportunity to obtain a new lamp in place of her husband's old one, and without knowing what she did, gave the magic lamp to the merchant, and received a new one in return. The merchant rubbed his ring on the magic lamp, and the fairy obeyed the summons, and desired to know what he wanted. He said, "Convey the castle as it stands with the princess in it, to my own country," and instantly his wish was gratified.

When the raja and his son-in-law returned from the chase, they were surprised and alarmed to find that the palace with its fair occupant had vanished, and had not left a trace behind. The dewan reminded his master that he had tried to dissuade him from rashly giving his daughter in marriage to an unknown person, and had foretold that some calamity was sure to follow. The raja being grieved and angry at the loss of his daughter, sent for her husband, and said to him, "I give you thirteen days during which to find my daughter. If you fail, on the morning of the fourteenth, I shall surely cause you to be executed." The thirteenth day arrived, and although her husband had sought her every where, the princess had not been found. Her unhappy husband resigned himself to his fate, saying, "I shall go and rest, to-morrow morning I shall be killed." So he climbed to the top of a high hill, and lay down to sleep upon a rock. At noon he accidentally rubbed his finger ring upon the rock on which he lay, and a fairy issued from it, and awaking him, demanded what he wanted. In reply he said, "I have lost my wife and my palace, if you know where they are, take me to them." The fairy immediately transported him to the gate of his castle in the merchant's country, and then left him to his own devices. Assuming the form of a dog, he entered the palace, and the princess at once recognized him. The merchant had gone out on business, and had taken the lamp with him, suspended by a chain round his neck. After consultation, it was determined that the princess should put poison in the merchant's food that evening. When he returned, he called for his supper, and the princess set before him the poisoned rice, after eating which he quickly died. The rightful owner repossessed himself of the magic lamp, and an application of the ring brought out the attendant fairy who demanded to know why he had been summoned. "Transport my castle with the princess and myself in it back to the king's country, and place it where it stood before," said the young man; and instantly the castle occupied its former position. So that before the morning of the fourteenth day dawned, not only had the princess been found, but her palace had been restored to its former place. The raja was delighted at receiving his daughter back again. He divided his kingdom with his son-in-law, giving him one-half, and they ruled the country peacefully and prosperously for many years.

The Two Brothers, Jhorea, and Jhore

There were two brothers, whose parents died, leaving them orphans when very young. The name of the elder was Jhorea, and of the younger Jhore. On the death of their parents, the two brothers went to seek employment, which they found in a certain village, far from where their home had been. The elder, Jhorea, was engaged as a farm servant, and the younger, Jhore, as village goat-herd.

After some time, it so happened that one day the brothers had no rice for their dinner, and Jhorea said to his brother, "Go to the owners of the goats you herd, and ask them for the hire they promised you. One will give you a pai, another a pawa, and a third a paila, and so on, according to the number of animals they have in your charge; some will give you more and others less, bring what you get, and cook some for dinner." The boy went as he was ordered, and entering the first house he came to, said, "Give me a pai." They said: "What do you want with a pai?" "Never mind what I want with it, give it," he replied. So they gave him a pai. Then he went to another house and said, "Give me a pawa." "What do you want with a pawa?" they said. "Never you mind, give it to me," and they gave him a pawa. He then went to a third house and asked for a paila. "What do you want with a paila?" they enquired. "Never you mind, give it to me," he replied. Instead of bringing rice he brought the wooden measures, and breaking them into small pieces, put them into the pot to cook. The elder brother was ploughing, and being very hungry, he kept calling out, "Cook the rice quickly, cook the rice quickly." His brother being impatient, he stirred the contents of the pot with all his might, at the same time exclaiming, "What can be the matter brother? it is very hard." The elder brother came to see what was wrong, and on looking into the pot saw only pieces of wood. He became very angry, and said, "I sent you to bring rice, why did you bring measures?" To which he replied, "You told me to ask a pai from one, a pawa from another, and a paila from a third, and I did so."

The elder then said to the younger, "You go and plough, and if the plough catch in a root on the right hand, cut the root on the left hand, and if it catch in a root on the left side, cut the root on the right side, and in the meantime I will cook." He went and began to plough, and in a short time the plough caught in a root on the right, and not understanding the directions given to him, he struck the left hand bullock a blow on the leg with his axe. The bullock limped along a short distance. When the plough caught in a root on the left, he smote the bullock on the right, wounding it as he had done the other. Both of the bullocks then lay down, and although he beat them they did not get up. He therefore called to his brother, "These bullocks have lain down, and will not get up, what shall I do?" "Beat them," was the reply. Again he beat them, but with no better result. The elder brother then came, and found that the oxen had been maimed, and were unable to stand, at which he became greatly alarmed, and said, "Why did you maim the oxen? The owners will beat us to death to-day." He then gave him some parched grain to eat, and sent him to look after his goats. The sun being hot, the goats were lying in the shade chewing their cud. He sat down near them, and began to eat the parched grain. Seeing the goats moving their jaws as if eating, he said, "These goats are eating nothing, they are lying there mocking me," and becoming enraged, he killed them all with his axe. Then going to his brother, he said, "Oh! brother, I have killed all the goats." His brother asked, "Why did you kill them?" He replied, "While I was watching them and eating the parched grain which you gave me, I saw them chewing, and as they were eating nothing I knew they were mocking me, and so I killed them all." The elder brother became greatly alarmed, and calling to the younger to come, they quickly ate their dinner, and then went to where the goats were lying dead. From among them they chose the fattest, and carried it off to the jungle, where they flayed, and cut it into pieces.

Jhore then said, "I shall take the stomach as my share," but his brother said, "No, let us take the flesh." Jhore, however, would not agree to that, and at length his brother said, "Well you take the stomach, I shall take the flesh." So each took what he fancied most, and they set off. After travelling a long distance, they came to a large tree growing on the side of the road, into which they climbed for safety. After they had been some time on the tree, a raja on his way to be married, lay down to rest in its shade, and when he and his attendants had fallen asleep, Jhore let the goat's stomach fall down on the raja. The raja having his rest thus rudely disturbed, sprang to his feet, and calling out, awoke his servants, who seeing the goat's stomach, and not knowing what had happened, thought the raja himself had burst. They fled in terror followed by the raja, and did not halt till they were many miles away from the scene of the raja's discomfiture.

After waiting a little while, the brothers descended, and began to help themselves to the raja's property. Jhore said, "I shall take the drum." His brother said, "No, let us take the brass vessels and the clothes." Jhore, however, insisted, and after considerable wrangling, his brother said, "Well, take the drum if you will have it, I shall take the brass vessels and the clothes." So each took what pleased him best, and then they went away and hid in the jungle.

While walking about in the jungle, they collected bees, wasps, and other stinging insects, and put them into the drum. Having filled the drum, they emerged from the forest at a place where a washerman was washing clothes. Jhore tore all his clothes into strips, and scattered them about. The washerman went and told the raja that two persons had come out from the jungle, and had destroyed all his clothes. On hearing this, the raja said to his servants, "Come, and let us fight with these two men." So arming themselves with guns, they went to the tank where Jhorea and Jhore were sitting, and began to shoot at them, but the bullets did them no harm. When their ammunition was exhausted, they said, "Will you still fight?" The brothers answered, "Yes, we will fight." So they began to fire their guns, and beat their drum, and the bees and wasps issued from it like a rope, and began to sting the raja and his soldiers, who to save themselves, lay down and rolled on the ground. The raja, in anguish from the stings of the bees, exclaimed, "I will give you my daughter, and half of my kingdom, if you will call off the bees." Hearing this they beat the drum, and calling to the bees and wasps, ordered them all to enter the drum again, and the raja and his people went to their homes. The brothers however, could not agree as to who should marry the princess. One said, "You marry her." The other said, "No, you marry her." The younger at length said to the elder, "You are the elder, you should take her, as it is not fitting that you should

beg. If I were to marry her, I could no longer go about begging."
So the elder brother married the princess, and became the raja's
son-in-law.

The two settled down there, and cultivated all kinds of crops. One
day the elder brother sent his younger brother to bring a certain
kind of grain. Taking a sickle and a rope to tie his sheaves with,
he went to the field. Arrived there, he found that the grain was
covered with insects. So he set fire to it, and while it was burning
he kept calling out, "Whoever desires to feast on roasted insects,
let him come here." When his brother knew what he had done, he
reprimanded him severely.

Some time afterwards, when the black rice was ripe, he again
ordered him to go and reap some, so getting a sickle, and rope to
bind his sheaves with, he went to the rice field. On looking about
to see where he would begin, he discovered that each stalk of rice
was covered with flies. "There is nothing here but flies. How can I
reap this?" Saying this, he set fire to the growing rice and burnt it
all to the ground. His brother, when he knew what had happened,
was very much displeased and threatened to beat him.

On another day he was sent to cut jari1 to make ropes, so taking
his sickle, he set off to the field of jari. As soon as he began to cut
the stalks, the seeds rattled in the pods, hearing which he stopped
and called out, "Who is calling me?" After listening awhile and
hearing nothing he began again, and the same noise issuing from
the plant he was cutting, he said, "These plants are remonstrating
with me for cutting them." So being offended, he set fire to and
burnt down the whole crop of *jari*[1].

---

[1] *Jari* is the Santali name for Crotalaria Juncea, a fibre yielding plant the seeds of which
when ripe, rattle in the pods when the plant is shaken.

On being informed of his brother's action, Jhorea seized a stick, and ran after him to beat him, but could not overtake him. In the direction Jhore was running, there were some men flaying an ox, and Jhorea called to them to lay hold of his brother. They could not, however, accomplish this, but as he passed, they threw the stomach of the ox at him, which he caught in his arms and carried away with him. Finding a drain that was open at both ends, he crept in at one end, and passed out at the other, but left the ox's stomach behind him. His brother soon arrived at the drain, and thinking he was still there, tried to drive him out by pushing in a stick, the sharp point of which perforated the ox's stomach. On withdrawing the stick, and seeing the contents of the ox's stomach adhering to it, he thought he had pierced and killed his brother, but he having passed out at the other end had run swiftly home, and hid himself among the rafters of the house. Jhorea returned home weeping, and immediately began to make the preparations necessary for Jhore's funeral ceremonies. He caused a sumptuous feast to be got ready, and invited all his relations and friends. When they were all assembled, he went into the house to offer Jhore his portion. Presenting it, he said: "Oh! my brother Jhore, I offer this to you, take it, and eat it." Jhore, from among the rafters said, "Give it to me brother, and I shall eat it." His brother, not expecting an answer, was alarmed, and fled to his friends without, exclaiming, "Do the spirits of dead men speak? Jhore's speaks."

It now being dark, Jhore descended from his perch, and taking up the food which had been cooked for his funeral feast, left the house by another door. Passing on to the high way, he kept calling out, "Travellers by the road, or dwellers in the jungle, if you require food, come here." Some thieves hearing him, said, "Come, let us go and ask some." So going to him they said, "Give us some too, Jhore." But he replied, "It is for me alone." On their asking a second time, he give it to them. After they had eaten it all, they said to him, "Come, let us go a thieving." So they went to a house, and while the thieves were searching for money, Jhore went and picked up small pieces of pottery, and tied them up in his cloth. When they met afterwards, seeing Jhore's bundle of what appeared like rupees, they said, "You were not with us, where did you get the money?" Opening his parcel, he shewed them the pieces of pottery, seeing which they said, "We will not have you as our comrade." He replied, "Then return the food which you ate." As they could not comply, they agreed to take him with them. Jhore then said, "Where shall we go now?" They replied, "To steal cloth." So they went to a house, and while the robbers were searching for cloth, Jhore began to pull the clothes from off the sleeping inmates. This awoke them, and starting up, they began to call loudly for help. The thieves made off, and Jhore with them. Seeing Jhore had spoiled their game, they said to him, "We will not allow you to go with us again." He said, "Then give me back the food you ate." Not being able to do so, they said, "Well, we will allow you to accompany us this once." Jhore then said, "What shall we steal now?" The thieves answered, "We shall now go to steal horses." So they went to a stable, and each of the thieves helped himself to a horse; but Jhore going behind the house, found a large tiger which he saddled and mounted. The thieves also mounted each on the horse he had stolen. As they rode along, Jhore's tiger sometimes went first, and sometimes the thieves' horses. When the thieves were in front, Jhore's tiger bit and scratched their horses, so they said to him, "You ride first, we shall follow." But Jhore said, "No, my horse is a Hindu horse, he cannot run in front, your horses are Santal horses, they run well and straight, so you ride ahead." When day began to dawn, Jhore's tiger evinced a tendency to leave the road and take to the jungle, but Jhore holding him in, exclaimed, "Ha! ha! my Hindu steed, ha! ha! my Hindu steed." When it was fully light, the tiger ran into the jungle, and Jhore got caught in the branch of a tree, and continued dangling there for some days.

It so happened that one morning a demon passing that way spied Jhore dangling from the tree, and seizing him, put him in a bag and carried him away. Being thirsty, he laid the bag down, and went to a spring to drink. While he was absent, Jhore got out of the bag, and putting a stone in instead, ran away. The demon having quenched his thirst, returned, and lifting the bag carried it home. His daughter came to welcome him, and he said to her, "Jhore is in the bag, cook him, and we shall have a feast." He then went to invite his friends to share it with him. When the demon's daughter had opened the bag, she found the stone, and was angry, because her father had deceived her. In a short time her father returned, bringing a large number of jackals with him. He said to her, "Have you cooked Jhore?" She replied, "Tush! tush! you brought me a stone."

The demon was highly incensed at having been outwitted, and exclaimed, "I will track Jhore till I find him, and this time I shall bring him home without laying him down." He then left, and before long found Jhore swinging in the same branch as before. Catching hold of him, he put him into a bag, the mouth of which he tied. This time he brought him home without once laying him down. Calling to his daughter, he said, "Cook Jhore, while I go to invite my friends." She untied the bag, and took Jhore out, and seeing his long hair, she said, "How is it that your hair has grown so long?" "I pounded it in the dhenki," he replied, "Will you pound mine, so that it may become long like yours," said the demon's daughter. Jhore replied, "I shall do so with pleasure, put your head in the dhenki, and I shall pound it." So she put in her head, and he pounded it so that he killed her. He then possessed himself of all her jewellery, and dressing in her clothes, cooked her body.

When the demon returned, accompanied by his friends, he said, "Well! daughter, have you cooked Jhore?" Jhore replied, "Yes, I have cooked him." On hearing this, the demon and the jackals who had come with him, were delighted, and setting to, they devoured the body of the demon's daughter.

After some days, the demon went to visit a friend, and Jhore divesting himself of the demon girl's clothes, went to where the demon had at first found him, and began to swing as before. Presently a tigress approached him and said, "Oh! brother, the hair of my cubs has grown very long, I wish you to shave them to-day." Jhore replied, "Oh! sister, boil some water, and then go to the spring to bring more." The tigress having boiled the water, went to the spring. While she was away, Jhore poured the boiling water over the two cubs, and scalded them to death. He made them grin by fixing the lips apart, and propped them up at the door of the tigress' house. On her return as she drew near, she saw her cubs, as she fancied, laughing, and said to herself. "They are delighted because their uncle has shaved them." Setting down her water pot, she went to look at them, and found them dead. Just then the demon came up, and she asked him, "Whom are you seeking to-day uncle?" He replied "I am seeking Jhore, he has caused me to eat my own daughter. Whom are you seeking?" The tigress replied, "I also am seeking Jhore; he has scalded my cubs to death."

The two then went in search of Jhore. They found him in a lonely part of the forest preparing birdlime, and said to him, "What are you doing, Jhore?" He replied, "I look high up, and then I look deep down." They said, "Teach us to do it too." He answered,

"Only I can do it." They asked him a second time, and received the same reply. On their begging him a third time to teach them, he said, "Well, I shall do it." He then put some of the birdlime into their eyes, and fixed their eyelids together, so that they could not open them. While they were washing their eyes, he ran away. As soon as they had rid themselves of the birdlime, they followed him and found him distilling oil from the fruit of the marking-nut tree. They said to him, "What are you doing, Jhore?" He replied, "I look deep down, and then high up." They said, "Teach us also." He replied, "Only I can do it." They asked him again, and he said, "Well I will do it." He then poured some of the oil he had distilled into their eyes. It burned them so, that they became stone-blind.

Jhore was next seen seated in a fig-tree eating the fruit. Some cattle merchants, passing under the tree with a large herd of cattle, saw him eating the figs, and asked him what it was he was eating. He replied, "Beat the bullock that is going last, and you shall find it." So they beat the bullock till it fell down. In the meantime, the herd had gone on ahead, and Jhore running after them drove them to his own house. His brother seeing the large herd of cattle, asked to whom they belonged. Jhore replied, "They are Jhore's property." Jhorea then said, "I killed my brother Jhore, what Jhore is it?" He made answer, "Your brother Jhore whom you thought you had killed." Jhorea was delighted to find his brother alive, and said to him, "Let us live together after this." So they lived peacefully together ever after.

The Boy and his Stepmother

A certain boy had charge of a cow which he used to tend while grazing. One day the cow said to him, "How is it that you are becoming so emaciated?" The boy replied, "My stepmother does not give me sufficient food." The cow then said to him, "Do not tell any one, and I will give you food. Go to the jungle and get leaves with which to make a plate and cup." The boy did as he was ordered, and behold, the cow from one horn shook boiled rice into the leaf plate, and from the other a relish for the rice into the cup. This continued daily for a considerable time, until the boy became sleek and fat.

The stepmother came to know of the relation which existed between the cow and her herd-boy, and to be revenged upon them she feigned illness. To her attendants she said, "I cannot possibly live." They asked, "What would make you live?" She replied, "If you kill the cow, I will recover." They said, "If killing the cow will cure you, we will kill it." The boy hearing that the life of the cow which supplied him with food was threatened, ran to her and said, "They are about to kill you." Hearing this the cow said, "You go and make a rope of rice straw, make some parts thick, and some thin, and put it in such a place as they can easily find it. When they are about to kill me, you seize hold of my tail and pull." The next day they proceeded to make arrangements to kill the cow, and finding the rope prepared by the boy the day before, they tied her with it to a stake. After she was tied the boy laid hold of her tail, and pulled so that the rope by which she was secured was made taut. A man now raised an axe, and felled her by a blow on the forehead. As the cow staggered the rope broke, and she and the boy were borne away on the wind, and alighted in an unexplored jungle. From the one cow other cows sprang, in number equal to a large herd, and from them another large herd was produced. The boy then drove his two herds of cows to a place where they could graze, and afterwards took them to the river to drink. The cows having quenched their thirst, lay down to rest, and the boy bathed, and afterwards combed and dressed his hair. During this latter operation a hair from his head fell into the river, and was carried away by the current.

Some distance lower down, a princess with her female companions and attendants came to bathe. While the princess was in the water she noticed the hair floating down stream, and ordered some one to take it out, which when done they measured, and found it to be twelve cubits long. The princess on returning home went to the king, her father, and showing him the hair she had found in the river said, "I have made up my mind to marry the man to whom this hair belonged." The king gave his consent, and commanded his servants to search for the object of his daughter's affection. They having received the king's command went to a certain barber and said to him, "You dress the hair and beards of all the men in this part of the country, tell us where the man with hair twelve cubits long is to be found." The barber, after many days, returned unsuccessful. The king's servants after a long consultation as to whom they should next apply to, decided upon laying the matter before a tame parrot belonging to the king. Going to the parrot they said, "Oh parrot, can you find the man whose hair is twelve cubits long?" The parrot replied, "Yes, I can find him." After flying here and there the parrot was fortunate enough to find the boy. It was evening, and having driven his two herds of cattle into their pen, he had sat down, and was employed in dressing his long hair. His flute was hanging on a bush by his side.

The parrot sat awhile considering how she might take him to the king's palace. Seeing the flute the idea was suggested to her, that by means of it she might contrive to lead him where she desired. So taking it up in her beak, she flew forward a little and alighted in a small bush. To regain possession of his flute the boy followed, but on his approach the bird flew away, and alighted on another bush a short distance ahead. In this way she continued to lead him by flying from bush to bush until at length she brought him to the king's palace. He was then brought before his majesty, and his hair measured, and found to be twelve cubits in length. The king then ordered food to be set before him, and after he was refreshed the betrothal ceremony was performed.

As it was now late they prevailed upon him to pass the night as the guest of the king. Early in the morning he set out, but, as he had a long distance to go, the day was far advanced before he reached the place where his cattle were. They were angry at having been kept penned up to so late an hour, and as he removed the bars to let them out, they knocked him down, and trampled upon his hair in such a way, as to pull it all out leaving him bald. Nothing daunted, he collected his cows, and started on his return journey, but us he drove them along, one after another vanished, so that only a few remained when he reached the king's palace.

On his arrival they noticed that he had lost all his hair, and on being questioned he related to the king all that had fallen him. His hair being gone the princess refused to marry him, so instead of becoming the king's son-in-law, he became one of his hired servants.

The Story of Kara and Guja

There were two brothers named Kara and Guja. Guja, who was the elder did the work at home, and Kara was ploughman.

One day the two went to the forest to dig edible roots. After they had been thus engaged for some hours, Kara said to Guja, "Look up and see the sun's position in the heavens." Looking up he said, "Oh brother, one is rising and another is setting." They then said, "The day is not yet past, let us bestir ourselves, and lose no time." So they dug with all their might.

After digging a long time Kara looked up and became aware that it was night. He then exclaimed, "Oh brother, it is now night, what shall we do? Come let us seek some place where we can remain until the morning." After they had wandered awhile in the forest they spied a light in the distance, and on drawing near they found that a tiger had kindled a fire, and was warming himself. Going up to the entrance to the cave they called out to the tiger, "Oh uncle, give us a place to sleep in." He answered, "Come in." So the two went in, and being hungry began to roast and eat the roots they had brought with them. The tiger hearing them eating, enquired what it was. They replied, "Oh uncle, we are roasting and eating the roots which we dug up in the forest." He then said, "Oh my nephews, I will also try how they taste." So they handed him a piece of charcoal, and as he munched it he said, "Oh my nephews, how is it that I feel it grating between my teeth?" They replied, "It is an old one that you have got, uncle." He then said, "Give me another, and I will try it." So they gave him another piece of charcoal, and after he had crunched it awhile he said, "Oh my nephews, this is as bad as the other," to which they rejoined, "Oh uncle, your mouth is old, therefore what is good to us, is the reverse to you." The tiger did not wish to try his grinders on another piece of charcoal, so the brothers were left to enjoy their repast alone.

After they had eaten all the roots, Guja said to Kara, "What shall we eat now? Come let us eat this old tiger's tail." Kara replied, "Do not talk in that way, brother, the tiger will devour us." "Not so, brother," said Guja, "I have a great desire to eat flesh." The old tiger understood their conversation, and being afraid tried to get out of the cave, but the brothers caught hold of him, and wrenched off his tail, which they roasted in the ashes, and then ate.

The tiger after losing his tail summoned a council of all the tigers inhabiting that part of the forest, at which they decided to kill and eat the two brothers. So they went to the cave, but Kara and Guja had fled, and had taken refuge in a palm tree which grew on the edge of a large deep tank. Not finding them in the cave the tigers, headed by him who had lost his tail, went in quest of them, and coming to the tank saw them reflected in the water, and one after another they dived in, thinking they would be able to seize them, but of course they could not catch a shadow.

One of the tigers, when in the act of yawning, looked upwards, and seeing them in the tree exclaimed, "There they are. There they are." They then asked the brothers how they had managed to climb up, to which they replied, "We stood on each other's shoulders." The tigers then said, "Come, let us do the same, and we shall soon reach them." As the tailless tiger was most interested in their capture, they made him stand lowest, and a tiger climbed up and stood on his shoulders, and another on his, and so on; but before they reached the brothers, Kara called out to Guja, "Give me your sharp battle-axe, and I shall hamstring the tailless tiger." The tailless tiger forgetting himself jumped to one side, and the whole pillar of tigers fell in a heap on the ground. They now began to abuse the old tailless tiger, who fearing lest they should tear him in pieces fled into the forest.

After the tigers had left, the two brothers descended from the palm tree, and walked rapidly away as they dreaded that the tigers might yet follow them. Towards evening they came to a village, and entering into the house of an old woman lay down to sleep. The owner of the house observing them said, "Oh my children, do not sleep to-night, for there is a demon who visits in rotation each house in the village, and each time he comes carries off some one and eats him; it is my turn to receive a visit to-night." They said, "Do not trouble us now, let us sleep, as we are tired." So they slept, but kept their weather eye open. During the night the old woman came quietly, and began to bite their arms, which they had laid aside before retiring to rest. Hearing a sound as if some one were crunching iron between his teeth, the brothers called out, "Old woman, what are you eating?" She replied "Only a few roasted peas which I brought from the chief's house." About midnight the demon came, and as he was entering the house Kara and Guja shot at him with their bows and arrows, and he fell down dead. Then they cut out his claws and tongue, and placed them in a bag.

Afterwards they threw out the body of the demon into the garden behind the house.

Now it so happened that the king had promised to give his daughter and half of his kingdom to the man who should slay the demon. Early in the morning a Dome, who was passing, discovered the body of the demon, and said within himself, "I will take it to the king and claim the reward." So running home he broke all the furniture in his house and beat his old woman saying, "Get out of this. I am about to bring the king's daughter home as my bride." He then returned quickly, and taking up the body of the demon carried it to the king, and said, "Oh sir king, I have slain the demon." The king replied, "Very well, we will enquire into it." So he commanded some of his servants to examine the body, and on doing so they found that the claws had been extracted and the tongue cut out. They reported the condition of the body to the king, who ordered the Dome to state the weapon with which he killed him. The Dome replied, "I hit him with a club on the head." On the head being examined no mark whatever was seen, so in order to arrive at the truth the king ordered all the inhabitants of the village to be brought together to the palace. He then enquired of them as to who killed the demon.

The old woman, in whose house Kara and Guja had passed the night, stepped forward and said, "Oh sir king, two strangers came to my house yesterday evening, and during the night they slew the demon." The king said, "Where are those two men?" The old woman replied, "There they are, the two walking together." So the king sent and brought them back, and questioned them as to the slaying of the demon. They pointed out the arrow-marks on the body, and produced his claws and tongue from their bag. This evidence convinced the king that they, and not the Dome, had slain the demon. Kara and Guja were received with great favour by the king, and received the promised reward.

The king sentenced the Dome to be beaten and driven from the village. After receiving his stripes, the Dome returned home, and gathered the shreds of his property together. He also went in search of his Dome wife and children, but they mocked him saying, "You went to marry the king's daughter, why do you come again seeking us."

Thus Kara and Guja gained a kingdom.

The King and his Inquisitive Queen

There was a certain king known by the name of Huntsman, on account of his expertness in the chase. One day when returning from the forest where he had been hunting he found a serpent and a lizard fighting on the path along which he was moving. As they were blocking the way he ordered them to stand aside and allow him to pass, but they gave no heed to what he said. King Huntsman then began to beat them with his staff. He killed the lizard, but the serpent fled, and so escaped.

The serpent then went to Monsha, the king of the serpents, and complained of the treatment the lizard and himself had received at the hands of king Huntsman. The next day king Monsha went and met king Huntsman on his way home from the forest, and blocked his way so that he could not pass. King Huntsman being angry said, "Clear the way, and allow me to pass, or else I shall send an arrow into you. Why do you block my way?" King Monsha replied, "Why did you assault the lizard and the serpent, with intent to kill them both?" King Huntsman answered, "I ordered them to get out of my way, but they would not, I therefore assaulted them, and killed one. The other saved himself by flight." King Monsha hearing this explanation said, "Very good, the fault was theirs, not yours."

King Huntsman then petitioned the king of the serpents to bestow upon him the gift of understanding the language of animals and insects. King Monsha acceded to his request, and gave him the gift he desired.

A few days after this event King Huntsman went to the forest, and after hunting all day returned home in the evening Having washed his hands and feet, he sat down to his meal of boiled rice. When the rice was being served to the king a few grains fell on the ground, and a fly and an ant began to dispute as to who should carry them away. The fly said, "I will take them to my children." The ant replied, "No, I will take them to mine." Hearing the two talk thus, the king was amused, and began to smile. The queen, who was standing by, said to him, "Tell me what has made you laugh." On being thus addressed the king became greatly confused, for at the time the gift of understanding the language of animals and insects was bestowed upon him, King Monsha had forbidden him to make it known to any one. He had said, "If you tell this to any one, I shall eat you." Remembering this the king feared to answer the question put to him by the queen. He tried to deceive her by saying, "I did not laugh, you must have been mistaken." She would not, however, be thus put off, so the king was obliged to tell her that if he answered her question his life would be forfeited. The queen was inexorable, and said, "Whether you forfeit your life or not, you must tell me." The king then said, "Well, if it must be so, let us make ready to go to the bank of the Ganges. There I shall tell you, and when I have done so you must push me into the river, and then return home."

The king armed himself, and the two set out for the river. When they had reached it, they sat down to rest under the shade of a tree. A flock of goats was grazing near to where they were seated, and the king's attention was arrested by a conversation which was being carried on between an old she-goat and a young he-goat. The former addressed the latter thus, "There is an island in the middle of the Ganges, and on that island there is a large quantity of good sweet grass. Get the grass for me, and I shall give you my daughter in marriage." The he-goat was not thus to be imposed upon. He angrily addressed his female friend as follows, "Do not think to make me like this foolish king, who vainly tries to please a woman. He has come here to lose his own life at the bidding of one. You tell me to go and bring you grass out of such a flood as this. I am no such fool. I do not care to die yet. There are many more quite as good as your daughter."

The king understood what passed between them, and admitted to himself the truth of what the he-goat had said. After considering a short time he arose, and having made a rude sacrificial altar, said to the queen, "Kneel down, and do me obeisance, and I shall tell you what made me laugh." She knelt down, and the king struck off her head and burnt her body upon the altar. Returning home he performed her funeral ceremonies, after which he married another wife.

He reigned prosperously for many years, and decided all disputes that were brought before him by animals or insects.

The Story of Bitaram

In a certain village there lived seven brothers. The youngest of them planted a certain vegetable, and went every day to examine it to see how it was growing. For a long time there were only the stalk and leaves, but at length a flower appeared, and from it a fruit. This fruit he measured daily to mark its growth. It grew continuously until it became exactly a span long, after which it remained stationary. One day he said to his sisters-in-law, "Do not eat my fruit, for whoever does so will give birth to a child only one span long." He continued his daily visits to his plant as usual, and was pleased to note that the fruit was evidently ripening. One day, during his absence, one of his sisters-in-law plucked the fruit and ate it. On returning from the field where he had been ploughing, he went to look at and measure his fruit, but it was gone, it had been stolen. Suspecting that some one of his sisters-in-law was the thief, he accused each of them in turn, but they all denied having touched it. When he found that no one would confess to having taken it, he said to them, "Do not tell upon yourselves, the thief will be caught before long." And so it happened, for one of them gave birth to a baby one span long. The first time he saw his sister-in-law after the child was born he laughed, and said to her, "You denied having stolen my fruit, now you see I have found you out."

When the time came that the child should receive a name, Bitaram[1] was given to him, because he was only a span in height. Bitaram's mother used to take food to the brothers to the field when they were ploughing, and when Bitaram was able to walk so far he accompanied her. One day he surprised his mother by saying, "Let me take the food to my father and uncles to-day." She replied, "What a fancy! You, child, are only a span high, how can you carry it?" But Bitaram insisted saying, "I can carry it well enough, and carry it I will." His mother being unable to resist his pertinacity said, "Then, child, take it, and be off." So she placed the basket on his head and he set out. Arrived at the field he went up a furrow, but the ground was so uneven that before he reached his destination, he had lost nearly all the rice, which had been shaken out of the basket. On his coming near, one of his uncles called out, "Is that you Bitaram?" He replied, "Yes, it is I, Bitaram." Climbing up out of the furrow, he put down the basket saying, "Help yourselves, and I will take the oxen and buffaloes to the water." So saying, he drove off the cattle to the river. When they had quenched their thirst he gathered them together, and began to drive them back again to where he had left his father and uncles. While following them up the sandy back of the river, he fell into a depression made by the hoof of a buffalo, and was soon covered up by the loose sand sent rolling down by the herd as they ascended.

When the cattle returned without Bitaram, his father and uncles became alarmed for his safety, and immediately went in search of him. They went here and there calling out "Bitaram, where are you?" But failing to find him they concluded that he had been

---

[1] Bita is Santali for span, and Bitaram is span Ram, or span-long Ram

devoured by some wild animal, and returned sorrowfully home. Rain fell during the night, and washed the sand from off Bitaram, so that he was able to get up, and climb out. On his way home he encountered some thieves who were dividing their booty in a lonely part of the forest. Bitaram hearing them disputing called out "Kehe kere" at the pitch of his voice. The thieves hearing the sound, looked round on all sides to see who was near, but the night being dark, and they not directing their eyes near enough to the ground to see Bitaram, they could discern no one. Then they said to each other, "Let us seek safety in flight. A spirit has been sent to watch us." So they all made off leaving behind them the brass vessels they had stolen. Bitaram gathered these up, and hid them among some prickly bushes, and then went home.

It was now past midnight, and all had retired to rest, and as Bitaram stood shivering with cold at the closed door, he called out, "Open the door and let me in." His father hearing him said, "Is that you Bitaram?" He replied, "Yes, open the door." They then enquired where he had been, and he related all that had happened to him after he had driven the cattle to the river. Having warmed himself at the fire, he told his father of his adventure with the thieves in the forest. He said, "I despoiled some thieves, whom I met in the jungle, of the brass vessels they had stolen." His father replied, "Foolish child, do not tell lies, you yourself are not the height of a brass lota" (drinking-cup). "No father," said Bitaram, "I am telling the truth, come and I will shew you where they are." His father and uncles went with him, and he pointed out to them the vessels hidden among the prickly bushes. They picked them all up and brought them home.

Early next morning some sepoys, who were searching for the thieves, happened to pass that way, and seeing the stolen property lying out side of the house, recognized it, and apprehended

Bitaram's father and uncles and dragged them off to prison. After this Bitaram and his mother were obliged to beg their bread from house to house. She often attributed to him the misery which had befallen them, saying, "Had it not been for your pertinacity, your father and uncles would not have been deprived of their liberty."

One day, as they were following their usual avocation, they entered a certain house, and Bitaram said to his mother, "Ask the people of the house to give me a tumki.[2]" She did not at first comply, but he kept urging her until being irritated she said, "It was through your pertinacity in insisting upon being allowed to carry the food to your father and uncles that they are now bound and in prison, and yet you will not give up the bad habit." Bitaram said, "No, mother, do ask it for me." As he would not be silenced she begged it for him, and the people kindly gave it.

At the next house they came to, they saw a cat walking about, and Bitaram said, "Oh mother, ask the people to give me the cat." As before, she at first refused, but he continued to press her, and she becoming annoyed scolded him saying, "The young gentleman insists on obtaining this and that. It was your pertinacity that caused your father and uncles to be dragged to prison in bonds." Bitaram replied, "Not so, mother, do ask them to give me the cat." As the only way to silence him she said to the people of the house, "Give my boy your cat, he will hold it in his arms for a few minutes, and then set it down, but he carried it away with him." Bitaram then begged his mother to make him a bag, and fill it with flour, saying, "I am going to obtain the release of my father and uncles." She mockingly replied, "Much you can do." She made him a bag, however, and filling it with flour said, "Be off."

---

[2] A small basket with a contracted opening.

Bitaram then strapped the bag of flour on the cat's back as a saddle, and mounted. Puss, however, refused to go in the direction desired, and it was with great difficulty that he prevailed upon her to take the road. As he rode along he observed a swarm of bees on an ant hill, and dismounting he addressed them as follows, "Come bees, go in, come bees, go in." The bees swarmed into the tumki, and Bitaram having covered them up with a leaf continued his journey. Before he had gone far he came to a large tank, which belonged to the raja who had imprisoned his father. A number of women had come to the tank for water, and Bitaram taking his stand upon the embankment began to shoot arrows at their waterpots. After he had broken several, the women espied him mounted on his cat with his bow and arrows in his hand, and believing him to be an elf from the forest fled in terror to the city. Going to the raja they said "Oh raja, come and see. Some one is on the tank embankment. We do not know who or what he is, but he is only a span high." The raja then summoned his soldiers, and commanded them to take their bows and arrows, and go and shoot him whoever he was. The soldiers went within range, but although they shot away all their arrows, they failed to hit him. So returning to the raja they said, "He cannot be shot." Hearing this the raja became angry, and calling for his bow and arrows, went to the tank and began to shoot at Bitaram, but although he persevered until his right side ached with drawing the bow, he could not hit him.

When he desisted, Bitaram called out "Are you exhausted?" The raja answered "Yes." Then said Bitaram "It is my turn now," and taking the leaf from off the mouth of the basket called to the bees, "Go into the battle, bees." The bees issued from the basket like a black rope, and stung the raja and those who were with him. No way of escape offering, the raja called out to Bitaram, "Call off your bees, and I will give you the half of my kingdom and my daughter, and I will also set at liberty your father and uncles." Bitaram gathered the bees into the basket, and after his father and uncles had been released, took them back to the ant hill from whence he had brought them. On his return he wedded the princess and received half of her father's kingdom.

Bitaram and his wife lived happily together, and every thing they took in hand prospered, so that before long they were richer than the king himself. One great source of Bitaram's wealth was a cow which the princess had brought him as part of her dowry. Being envious of their good fortune, the raja and his sons resolved to kill the cow, and thus obtain possession of all the gold and silver. So they put the cow to death, but when they had cut her up they were disappointed as neither gold nor silver were found in her stomach.

Bitaram placed his cow's hide in the sun, and when it was dry carried it away to sell it. Darkness coming on he climbed into a tree for safety, as wild beasts infested the forest through which he was passing. During the night some thieves came under the tree in which he was, and began to divide the money they had stolen. Bitaram then relaxed his hold of the dry hide, which made such a noise as it fell from branch to branch that the thieves fled terror-stricken, and left all their booty behind them. In the morning Bitaram descended, and collecting all the rupees carried them home. He then shewed the money to his wife, and said "Go and ask the loan of your father's paila, that I may measure them." So she went and brought the measure, which had several cracks in it. Having measured his money he sent back the raja's paila, but he had not noticed that one or two pieces were left sticking in the cracks. So they said to him, "Where did you get the money?"

He replied "By the sale of my cow's hide." Hearing this they said, "Will the merchant who bought yours, buy any more?" He said, "Yes. I received all this money for my one hide, how much more may not you receive seeing you have such large herds of cattle! If you dispose of their hides at the same rate as I have done, you will secure immense wealth." So they killed all their cattle, but when they offered the hides for sale they found they had been hoaxed. They were ashamed and angry at having allowed themselves to be thus imposed upon by Bitaram, and in revenge they set fire to his house at night, but he crept into a rat's hole and so escaped injury. In the morning he emerged from his hiding place, and carefully gathering up the ashes of his house tied them up in a cloth, and carried them away. As he walked along he met a merchant, to whom he said, "What have you in your bag?" He replied "Gold-pieces only." The merchant then enquired of Bitaram what he had tied up in his cloth, to which he answered, "Gold-dust only." Bitaram then said, "Will you exchange?" The merchant said, "Yes." So they exchanged, and Bitaram returned laden with gold. Not being able to count it, he again sent his wife to borrow her father's paila, and having measured the gold-pieces returned it to him. This time a few pieces of gold remained in the cracks in the paila, and the raja, being informed of it, went and asked Bitaram where he got the gold. He replied, "I sold the ashes of my house which you burnt over my head, and received the gold in return." The raja and his sons then enquired if the merchant, who bought the ashes from him, would buy any more. Bitaram replied, "Yes, he will buy all he can get." "Do you think," said they, "he will buy from us?" Bitaram advised them to burn their houses, and like him, turn the ashes into gold. "I had only one small house," he said, "and I obtained all this money. You have larger houses, and should therefore receive a correspondingly large amount." So they set fire to, and burnt their houses, and gathering up the ashes took them to the bazar, and there offered them for sale. After they had gone the whole length of the bazar, and had met with no buyers, some one advised them to go to where the washermen lived, saying, they might possibly take them. The washermen, however, refused, and as they could not find a purchaser, they threw away the ashes, and returned home determined to be revenged upon Bitaram.

This time they decided upon drowning him, so one day they seized him, and putting him into a bag they carried him to the river. Arrived there they put him down, and went to some little distance to cook their food. In the meantime a herd boy came up and asked Bitaram why he was tied up in the bag. He replied, "They are taking me away to marry me against my will." The herd boy said, "I will go instead of you. I wish to be married." Bitaram replied, "Open the bag and let me out, and you get in, and I will tie it up again." So Bitaram was released, and the herd boy took his place, and was afterwards thrown into the river and drowned.

Bitaram on escaping collected all the herd boy's cattle, and drove them home. When the raja and his sons returned, they found Bitaram with a large herd of cows and buffaloes. Going near, they enquired where he had got them. He replied, "At some distance below the spot where you threw me into the river, I found numerous herds of cattle, so I brought away as many as one person could drive. If you all go, you will be able to bring a very much larger number." So they said, "Very well, put us into bags, and tie us up as we did you." Bitaram replied, "It is impossible for me to carry you as you did me. Walk to the river bank, and there get into the bags, and I will push you into the river." They did as he suggested, and when all was in readiness, he pushed them into the river, and they were all drowned.

Bitaram returned alone, and took possession of all that had belonged to them. The whole kingdom became his, and he reigned peacefully as long as he lived.

The Story of Sit and Bosont

There was a certain raja who had two sons named Sit and Bosont. Their mother the rani had been long ill, and the raja was greatly dejected on her account. From the bed on which she lay, the rani could see two sparrows who had made their nest in a hole in the wall of the palace, and she had remarked the great love and tenderness which the hen-sparrow bore towards her young ones. One day she saw both sparrows sitting in front of their nest, and the sight of them set her a-thinking, and she came to the conclusion that the hen-sparrow was a model mother. The raja also had his attention attracted daily by the sparrows. One day, very suddenly, the hen-sparrow took ill, and died. The next day the cock-sparrow appeared with another mate, and sat in front of the nest with her, as he had done with the other. But the new mother took no notice of the young ones in the nest, but left them to die of hunger. The rani, who was greatly grieved to see such want of compassion, said to the raja, "This is how it is, one has no pity for those who belong to another. Remember what you have been a witness of, and should I die take care of the two children." Shortly after this the rani died, and the raja mourned over her, and continued most solicitous for the welfare of their two boys.

Some months after the rani's death, the raja's subjects prayed him to take another wife, saying, "Without a rani your kingdom is incomplete." The raja refused to comply, saying, "I shall never take another wife." His subjects would not, however, be silenced, but continued to press the matter upon him with such persistency that eventually he had to accede to their wishes, and take to himself another partner. He continued, however, to love and cherish his two sons Sit and Bosont.

Some time after their marriage the rani took a dislike to the elder son Sit, and was determined that he should no longer be allowed to remain within the precincts of the palace. So she feigned sickness, and the raja summoned physicians from all parts of his dominions, but without avail, as none of them could tell what the disease was from which the rani was suffering. One day when Sit and Bosont were out of the way, and the raja and she were alone together, she said to him, "Doctors and medicines will not save my life, but if you will listen to me, and do what I tell you, I shall completely recover." The raja said, "Let me hear what it is, and I shall try what effect it may have." The rani said, "If you will promise to do for me what I shall request, I will tell you, and not otherwise." The raja replied, "I shall certainly comply with your wishes." The rani again said, "Will you without doubt, do what I wish?" The raja replied, "Yes, I shall." After she had made him promise a third time she said, "Will you take oath that you will not seek to evade fulfilling my desire?" The raja said, "I take my oath that I shall carry out your wishes to the full extent of my ability." Having thus prevailed upon the raja to pledge his word of honour, she said, "Do not allow your eldest son, Sit, to remain any longer in the palace. Order him to leave, and go somewhere else, so that I may not see his face, and never to return."

On hearing this the raja was greatly distressed. But what could he do? The rani had said, "If you permit him to remain, I shall die, and if you fulfil my wishes I shall live," and in his anxiety to save the life of his rani, he had bound himself by an oath before he knew what it was he would be required to do. After much consideration as to how he could best communicate the order to leave the palace to his son, he decided to write it on a sheet of paper and fix it, during his absence, to the door of his room. When the brothers returned, they found the paper placed there by the raja, and on reading it, were greatly troubled. After some time, during which Sit had been considering the position in which he found himself, he said to his brother, "You must remain, and I must go." On hearing his brother's words, Bosont's heart was filled with sorrow, and he replied, "Not so, I cannot see you go away alone. You have been guilty of no fault for which our parents could send you away. I cannot remain here alone. I will accompany you. We are children of the same mother, and we should not part." His brother replied, "Let us leave the house to-day. We can pass the night in some place close at hand." So they left their father's house, and concealed themselves in its vicinity. On the approach of evening they began to feel the pangs of hunger, and the younger said to the elder, "What shall we do? We have no food." After a minute's thought, the elder replied, "Although we have been sent adrift, we will take our elephants, and horses, and clothes, and money along with us." So when night had fallen, they entered the palace and brought out all that belonged to them, and at cock-crow, set forth on their journey. They travelled all day, and as the sun began to decline, they reached a dense jungle, and passing through it they came to a large city where they put up for the night. The city pleased them much, and they hired quarters in the Sarai. After they had gained a little acquaintance with their surroundings, Sit, attired in gorgeous apparel, and mounted on a splendid horse, rode every evening through the principal streets of the city. One evening the daughter of the raja of that country, from the roof of the palace, saw him ride past, and fell deeply in love with him. She immediately descended to her room, and feigning sickness, threw herself upon her couch. Her parents, on entering, found her weeping bitterly, and on enquiring the cause were informed by her attendants that she had been suddenly seized with a dangerous illness, the nature of which they did not know. The raja at once summoned the most famed physicians that could be found, to cure his daughter. One after another, however, failed to understand her complaint, and she grew worse daily. She was heard continually wailing, "I shall never recover; I shall die." After the doctors had retired baffled, she addressed her parents as follows; "You, who gave me life, listen to my entreaty. There is one expedient still, which if you will agree to put into execution, I shall recover, and be as well as formerly, and should you refuse to do as I say, and call it foolishness, then you shall never see my face again, I shall depart this life at once." On hearing these words, her parents said, "Tell us, what it is, we will surely act agreeably to your wishes." She replied, "Oh! father, promise me that you will carry them out without reserve." Her parents then promised with an oath, that they would do all she desired. Then she told her story, "Of late we have daily seen a young man in dazzling white apparel, riding and curveting his horse through the city; if you betroth me to that young prince, I shall enjoy my accustomed health again."

On hearing this, her parents became greatly distressed, as they were averse to betrothing their daughter to a stranger of whom they knew nothing. After consulting together they said, "He comes this way in the evening, let us look out for him, and see what he is like." About sunset, Sit, mounted on his horse, rode in the direction of the palace. The raja had given orders to some of his attendants to arrest the man who, every evening dressed in white, rode past the palace. So, on his appearing, they laid hold of him and led him into the presence of the raja, who being pleased with his appearance, at once introduced him to his daughter's room. She, on beholding him, instantly became well, and that same evening the two were married.

Bosont having charge of the property remained in the Sarai, while his brother went out riding. Sit not returning at his usual time, Bosont was alarmed and waited anxiously for his return. At length, being wearied, he fell asleep. During the night a gang of thieves entered his room, and began to carry off all his valuables. Bosont slept so soundly that they had time to take away everything save his bed-clothes. To obtain possession of these they had to lift him, on which he awoke and gave the alarm. The thieves beat him with their clubs till he was half dead; then, senseless and with a broken leg, they threw him into the dry bed of a river.

In the morning his servants became aware of the robbery, and also that their master was missing. His groom found him some time after in the river bed, and carried him to a doctor who bound up his limb, and took care of him. He was soon well enough to move about, but doomed to halt through life.

The raja of that country was very wealthy, and had ships on the sea. Whenever a ship left the port on its outward voyage, it was customary to carry a man on board, who, on the rising of a storm at sea, was cast over board to appease to wrath of the Spirit of the mighty Deep. Without such a victim on board, no ship could leave the harbour. Now, it so happened that one of the raja's vessels was about to sail to a foreign port, but no man suitable for the sacrifice could be obtained. At last the raja ordered them to take the lame man, whom he had seen limping about the city. He, not knowing the purpose they had in view in asking him to accompany them on their voyage, gladly embraced the opportunity of seeing foreign lands. No sooner was he on board than the ship began to move, and to obtain a better view he climbed up the mast, and sat on the top of it. In twelve days they reached a port. Bosont, however, did not decend from his elevated station, but continued gazing on the country lying around.

The daughter of the raja of that city, while walking on the roof of the palace, enjoying the cool of the evening, saw Bosont seated on the ship's mast. She at once fell violently in love with him, and descending to her room, feigned sickness. Her parents called in the most famed physicians, but their skill was of no avail, the young lady's illness increased in intensity. At last, when her parents began to give up hope of saving her life, she said, "The doctors cannot do me any good, but if you will do as I direct you, I shall recover." They said, "Tell us what it is that we can do for you." She replied, "Before I can make it known to you, you must take oath that you will not seek to evade the performance of it." To this they agreed, and the princess said, "If you will betroth me to the man sitting on the top of the mast of the vessel in the harbour, I shall immediately regain my health." The raja despatched messengers to the ship, and had Bosont brought to the palace, and solemnized their marriage that same evening.

A few days after the above occurrence, the ship was ready to set sail on her homeward voyage, so they took the lame man on board, his wife also following. After they had been a few days at sea, the vessel was in danger of foundering in a storm. The sailors searched for the victim, but he could nowhere be found. At last one of the crew looking up, spied him seated on the mast and climbing swiftly up, pushed him into the sea. His wife had brought a tumba with her, and seeing her husband in the sea, threw it to him. With this assistance he was able to swim to the vessel, and laying hold of the stern, followed swimming all the way to port. When the vessel was brought to anchor, he climbed up into it, and disguised himself as a fakir. The people of the city noticed him daily walking on the shore in front of the ship, and believed him to be in reality a fakir.

One day the raja seeing Bosont's wife took a fancy to her, and caused her to be brought to his palace. She had apartments assigned to her in the best part of it, and was treated with great distinction. On the raja offering her marriage, she declined, saying, "Speak not to me of it." After several days the raja enquired, "Why do you still refuse to become my wife." She replied, "Ask the fakir who is always to be seen pacing the shore in front of a vessel lying in the harbour." The raja gave orders immediately to have the fakir brought to the palace. On his being ushered into his presence, the raja said, "What do you know regarding the woman, who on declining to be my wife, referred me to you for an explanation?" In reply Bosont related in the form of a fable, the history of Sit and himself, and also what befell him after they were parted from each other. Sit, who was now raja recognized his brother in the fakir before him, and falling on his neck, wept for joy. The two brothers continued ever after to live together.

The Story of a Tiger

certain man had charge of a number of cattle. One day he took them to graze near a quagmire, and leaving them there went in search of jungle fruits. It so happened that one of the bullocks was browsing on the edge of the quagmire when a tiger came creeping stealthily up, and sprang upon it, but somehow or other missed his mark, and fell into the quagmire and there stuck fast. When the herd come to drive his cattle home, he found the tiger fast in the mud, and called a large number of people to come and see him. The tiger addressed those who came to gaze upon him as follows, "Oh men, pull me out. I am in great straits." They replied, "We will not pull you out even to save your life. You are a ravenous animal." The tiger said, "I will not eat you." So they pulled him out. When he was again on dry land, he said, "I will devour you, for it is my nature to do so." They replied, "Will you really eat us?" "Yes, I will," said the tiger. "Well," they rejoined, "if you will devour us, what can we do to prevent you? But let us first ask the opinion of some others as to whether it is right for you to eat us or not." So they requested the opinion of all the trees in the forest, and each said, "Human beings are all bad." On asking the Mohwa tree, it replied, "Men are not good. Behold every year I give them my flowers to eat, and my fruit from which to make oil. In the hot weather I give them shade, and on leaving, when they have rested, they give me a parting slash with their axes, therefore it is right to eat these people, as they return evil for good." So said all the trees.

From this forest they went to another in which they found a cow to whom they said, "We are come to ask your opinion on a certain matter about which we are at variance. This tiger was up to the neck in a quagmire, and we pulled him out. Now he wishes to return evil for good. Is it right for him to do so?" The cow replied, "Yes, yes, I have heard what you have got to say. You human beings are not the correct thing. Behold me, how much I have contributed to the health and comfort of my master, yet he does not recognize my merit. Now that I am old, he has turned me out, and should I improve a little in condition, he will say, 'I will take this cow to the market and sell it. I will at least get a few pence for it.' Behold, when a man is well to do, he has many friends, but when he is poor, no one knows him. Verily, you are worthy to be devoured." The tiger then said to the men, "Well, have you heard all this? Are you convinced?" They said, "Hold on, let us ask one person more." So as they walked along they saw a jackal and called to him, "Oh uncle, stand still." The jackal said, "No I cannot wait, my companions, who are on their way to see the swinging festival, are far ahead of me, and I am hurrying to overtake them." They said to him, "Wait a little and settle this matter for us. We pulled this tiger out of a quagmire, and now he wishes to devour us." The jackal then said to the tiger, "Is this true? I cannot believe that a famed individual like yourself would be fool enough to jump into a quagmire. Come, shew me the place, and how it happened." So the tiger led him to the quagmire, and said, "This is the place from which I sprang, and this is how I did it," and he leaped into the quagmire. The jackal turning to the men, said, "What are you staring at? Pelt him with stones." So they all set to and stoned the tiger to death.

Story of a Lizard, a Tiger, and a lame Man

Once upon a time in a certain jungle, a lizard and a tiger were fighting, and a lame man, who was tending goats near by, saw them. The tiger being beaten by the lizard was ashamed to own it, and coming to the lame man said, "Tell me which of us won." The lame man being in great fear lest the tiger should eat him, said, "You won." On another occasion the lizard was compelled to flee, and took refuge in an ant hill. The tiger pursued him, but not being able to get him out, sat down to watch.

The lizard seeing his opportunity, crept stealthily up to his inveterate enemy, and climbing up his tail, fixed his teeth into his haunch, and held firmly on. The tiger felt the pain of the lizard's bite, but could not reach him to knock him off, so he ran to the lame man, and said, "Release me from this lizard." When he had caused the lizard to let go his grip, the tiger said, "Oh lame man, which of us won in the encounter?" The poor man in great fear said, "You won."

The same scene was enacted daily for many days. The tiger always came to the lame man and said, "Knock off this lizard," and after he had done so, would say, "Which of us won?" The lame man invariably replied, "You won." This had happened so often that the lame man began to feel annoyed at having to tell a lie every day to please the tiger. So one day after an ignominious flight on the part of the tiger, he being, as usual, requested to give his opinion as to who won, said, "The lizard had the best of it." On hearing this the tiger became angry, and said, "I shall eat you, my fine fellow, because you say the lizard defeated me. Tell me where you sleep." The poor lame man on hearing the tiger threaten him thus, trembled with fear, and was silent. But the tiger pressed him. He said, "Tell at once, for I shall certainly devour you." The lame man replied, "I sleep in the wall press." When night fell, the tiger set off to eat the lame man, but after searching in the wall press failed to find him. In the morning the lame man led his goats out to graze, and again met the tiger, who addressed him as follows, "You are a great cheat. I did not find you in the wall press last night." The lame man replied, "How is it you did not find me? I was sleeping there." "No," said the tiger, "you were not, you have deceived me. Now, tell me truly where you sleep." "I sleep on a rafter," said the lame man. About midnight the tiger went again in search of him to eat him, but did not find him on the rafter, so he returned home. In the morning the lame man as usual led his goats out to graze, and again encountered the tiger, who said to him, "How now! Where do you sleep? I could not find you last night." The lame man rejoined, "That is strange, I was there all the same." The tiger said, "You are a consummate liar. Now tell me plainly where you sleep at night, for I shall without doubt eat you." The lame man replied, "I sleep in the fire-place." Again the tiger went at night, but could not find him. Next morning he met the lame man, and said to him, "No more tricks, tell me where you sleep." He, thrown off his guard, said, "In the gongo."[1]

The tiger then withdrew to his den to wait till night came on, and the lame man, cursing his indiscretion, with a heavy heart, drove his goats homewards. Having made his charge safe for the night, he sat down feeling very miserable. He refused the food that was set before him, and continued bewailing his hard lot. In the hope of inducing him to eat, they gave him some mohwa wrapped in a sal leaf. This also failed to tempt him to eat; but he carried it with him when he crept into the gongo to sleep. At night the tiger came and lifting up the gongo felt it heavy, and said, "Well, are you inside?" He replied, "Yes, I am." So the tiger carried off the gongo with the lame man in it. By the time the tiger had gone a considerable distance, the lame man became hungry and said within himself, "I shall have to die in the end, but in the meantime I will appease my hunger." So he opened his small parcel of mohwa, and the dry leaf crackled as he did so. The noise frightened the tiger and he said, "What is it you are opening?" The lame man replied, "It is yesterday's lizard." "Hold! hold!" exclaimed the tiger, "Do not let him out yet, let me get clear away first." The lame man said, "Not so, I will not wait, but will let him out at once." The tiger being terrified at the prospect of again meeting his mortal enemy, the redoubtable lizard, threw down the gongo and fled, calling out, "I will not eat you. You have got the lizard with you."

In this way the lame man by means of the lizard saved his life.

---

[1] Covering for the head and shoulders made of leaves pinned together, worn as a protection from the rain by women, while planting rice.

The Story of a Simpleton

There was once a certain simpleton who had never seen a horse, but had heard that there was such an animal, and that men rode on his back. His curiosity was greatly excited, and he went here and there searching for a horse, so that he might ride on its back. On his way he fell in with a wag, and asked him, what horses were like, where they could be found, and whence were they produced. The wag replied, "They are very large, they are to be had at the weekly market, and they are hatched from eggs." He then asked, "What is the price of the eggs?" The other replied, "Price! They are cheap, one pice each." So one day he went to the market and bought four eggs which he saw exposed for sale, and brought them home with him. He then made preparations for a lengthened absence from his house, and started for the jungle, taking with him rice, a cooking pot and fire, to get the eggs hatched. Having reached the jungle, he placed the eggs to hatch in what turned out to be a tiger's den, and then went some distance off and sat down. After a short time he went to have a look at the eggs, and found one was missing. He was greatly distressed, at having as he fancied lost his horse, and cried out, "It has hatched, and run away somewhere. But what has happened, has happened. What can I do? I'll look out for the next one when it hatches." He then went to cook his rice, and returning after some time missed another of the eggs. He was very much grieved over the loss of the two eggs, and mourning his misfortune, cried, "Where have the two gone, after they came out of the shell? There still, however, remain two eggs." So saying, he returned to finish his cooking. After a few minutes' interval, he went to have a look at the eggs, and saw that another had disappeared; only one remained. His grief at the loss of three horses, was intense. He cried out, "Oh! where shall I find them? Three horses have been hatched, and they have all run away." He then went to where his cooking had been performed, and quickly ate his rice, and returned in all haste to look at his egg. It too was gone. On seeing this, his sorrow and disappointment were acute. He bemoaned his ill luck as follows, "After all the trouble I was at to procure my eggs, they have all hatched, and the horses are lost. But what is, must be. I shall relieve my mind by taking a chew of tobacco." After putting the tobacco into his mouth he noticed the tiger's den, and said, "It is in here, the horses have gone." So he went and broke from a tree a long stick with which he tried to poke his horses out. For some time his labours met with no reward, but at last he succeeded in forcing the tiger out of his den. Just as he was coming out, the simpleton by some chance or other got astride of his back, and called out, "At last I have found a horse." His delight was boundless. But the tiger would not go in the direction of his rider's house, but kept going further into the jungle. The simpleton then struck him about the head and ears saying, "As ghur ghur, as ghur ghur;"[1] nevertheless the tiger plunged deeper into the jungle. At last he bolted into a thicket of trailing plants, where he unseated the simpleton. The tiger having got rid of his rider fled. Afterwards he met a jackal who said to him, "Where away, in such hot haste?" "Uh!" he said, "how much of it can I tell

---

[1] Said to bullocks when ploughing to cause them to turn at the end of a furrow.

you! I have been greatly harassed, and distressed by As ghur ghur. It was with great difficulty I succeeded in giving him the slip, and now I am fleeing for dear life." The jackal said, "Come along and shew him to me, and I shall soon eat him up." The tiger replied, "Oh dear! no. I cannot go. If he finds me again he will do for me altogether." "Nonsense," said the jackal, "lead me to where he is, and I shall devour him." The tiger was persuaded, and led the way, and the jackal followed. After some little time they met a bear, who said, "Where are you two going?" The jackal gave answer, "This person has somewhere seen As ghur ghur and I am saying to him, 'Take me to where he is, and I shall eat him,' but he will not push ahead." Then the bear said, "Come let us all go together, and I shall eat him up." The tiger said, "I will go no further." The jackal then said, "Listen to me, I will put you upon a plan. Let us hold on by each other's tails, in this way you will have no cause to fear any evil." This suggestion pleased them well, and they cried out, "Yes, let us do that. You have hit upon a first rate expedient." Then the bear took hold of the tiger's tail, and the jackal that of the bear, and in this way they pursued their journey. But just as they drew near the thicket in which the simpleton had been left, the tiger exclaimed, "Look there, he is coming towards us," and being terribly frightened, fled at his utmost speed dragging the bear and jackal after him tearing the skin from off their bodies on the rough stones and gravel. At length the jackal cried out, "Hold on uncle, hold on uncle, you have rubbed all the skin off my body." But he would not halt, but kept dashing on through wood and brake, dragging them after him, until the bear's tail broke, and the jackal was released. His body by this time was all raw flesh, and he was swollen into a round mass. However, he managed to pick himself up, and run for his life.

Afterwards they met in with a pack of wild dogs who said, "Hulloo! what's up, that you are fleeing in such a plight?" They replied, "We are fleeing from As ghur ghur." "Where is he?" said they, "We will eat him." The tiger said, "There just in front of you, where you see the dark spot in the forest." So they went in the direction indicated, and while they were yet some distance off, they saw the simpleton standing in the shade of the trees. He also saw them, and being afraid hid himself in a hollow tree. On coming up to the tree in which he was, they surrounded it, and one of their number essayed to poke him out of his hiding place with his tail. The simpleton, however, taking hold of it twisted it round his hands, and pulled with all his might. The pain caused by his tail being pulled, caused the wild dog to grin. On seeing this, one of his companions said, "Oh! Brother, wherefore do you grin." He said, "I have got hold of him, and I am smiling with pleasure." The simpleton from within the tree continued to pull, till the tail of the wild dog broke, and he fell to the ground with a thud. The others on looking at him noticed that he had lost his tail. So they all became panic stricken, and fled from the place with all possible speed.

The simpleton took up his residence in that part of the jungle in which the above occurred. He is said to be the ancestor of the Bir hors, or jungle Santals.

A Thief and a Tiger

On a certain country there lived a very wealthy man whose cattle grazed on a wide plain. One day a tiger noticed them, and so did three thieves. At night the tiger came to where they were lying, and so did the three thieves, but the tiger arrived first. The night was pitch dark, and the cows getting frightened fled to their owner's premises, and all entered the cattle shed. When the tiger saw the cattle flee he ran after them, and entered the shed along with them. The thieves, coming to where they expected to find the cattle, and not seeing them, also went to the cattle shed; but the people of the house not having yet retired to rest, they hid themselves in the vicinity. When all became still, they entered the cattle shed, and began feeling for the largest and fattest oxen. Two of the thieves, each finding one to his mind, drove them away. But one man being more difficult to please than his neighbours continued to go from one to another groping for a good fat one. In this way he laid his hands on the tiger, it seemed a fat one, but lest there should be one still fatter, he left him for a little. However, as he did not find one better than the tiger he returned to him, and felt him all over again. He was without doubt the fattest in the shed, so he drove him out. On reaching the open field, the tiger went in the direction of the jungle, and his driver had great difficulty in getting him to go the road he wished. In this way,—the tiger going one direction, and the man pulling him another,—they spent the night. At cock-crow the thief became aware, that it was a tiger he had been contending with in the dark, and not an ox. He then said to the tiger, "It is you then, whom I have taken possession of." He then released the tiger, who fled to the jungle at full speed.

The thief having been awake all night felt tired, and lying down in the shade of a ridge of a rice field to rest, fell asleep.

The tiger as he ran encountered a jackal who exclaimed, "Ho! Ho! uncle, where are you off to, at such a break-neck pace?" The tiger replied, "I am going in this direction. A mite kept me awake all night, I am fleeing through fear of him." The jackal then said, "It is very strange, uncle, that you did not vanquish him. We eat such as he. Tell me where he is, and I shall soon snap him up." The tiger said, "He is over in the direction of those rice fields, asleep somewhere." The jackal then went in search of him, and soon found him asleep in the shade of a ridge of a rice field. He then went all round him reconnoitring, and when he had completed the circuit exclaimed, "The tiger said he was a mite, but he turns out to be of immense size, I cannot eat him all myself. I will gather my friends together to assist me, and then we shall devour him in no time." So he sat down with his back towards the sleeping thief, so near that his tail touched his neck, and began to yell as only a hungry jackal can. The noise awoke the sleeper, and seeing the jackal sitting so near to him, he quietly caught him by the tail, and springing on to his feet swung him round and round above his head, and then flung him from him. The jackal was severely stunned, but picking himself up, fled as fast as his legs could carry him. After he had gone some little distance he met a bear, who said, "Where away in such hot haste?" He made answer,

"Uh! What can I tell you more than that that barren tiger grossly deceived me. He told me he was a mite, I went to see him and found he was a *ghur pank*,[1] and without doubt he ghur panked me." The bear then said, "Oh! I'll eat him. Tell me where he is." The jackal said, "You will find him over in these rice fields." So the bear went to find him and eat him. When still some distance off he spied him laying asleep, and was greatly delighted, exclaiming, "My belly will be swollen with eating him before long." The thief accidentally lifted his head, and saw the bear coming straight for him, so he jumped up and ran to the nearest tree into which he climbed. The bear saw him, and went up after him, and tried to get hold of him, but he jumped from one branch to another as the bear followed him. After this had gone on for some time, it so happened that the bear missed his footing and fell heavily to the ground. The thief immediately jumped on to his back. The bear was frightened, and getting to his feet fled as fast as he could; the thief clasped him tightly round the neck, saying, "If I let go my hold he will eat me." The bear of course ran to the jungle, where the thief was caught by the branches of the trees, and dragged off his back. He did not return to the rice fields to sleep, as he feared some other animal might come to eat him, but went to his own home.

As the bear fled, he again met the jackal who asked him, "Well! did you eat him?" The bear replied, "You Sir, are a great cheat, you told me he was ghur pank. He is kara upar chap."[2] The two quarrelled over the matter, and the bear tried to catch the jackal to eat him, but he managed to escape.

---

[1] *Ghur pank* is a phrase used by ploughmen when turning their bullocks at the end of a furrow.
[2] Mount the buffalo.

The Magic Fiddle

Once upon a time there lived seven brothers and a sister. The brothers were married, but their wives did not do the cooking for the family. It was done by their sister. The wives for this reason bore their sister-in-law much ill will, and at length they combined together to oust her from the office of cook and general provider, so that one of themselves might obtain it. They said, "She does not go out to the fields to work, but remains quietly at home, and yet she has not the meals ready at the proper time." They then called upon their Bad Bonga,[1] and vowing vows unto him they secured his good will and assistance; then they said to the Bad Bonga, "At mid-day when our sister-in-law goes to bring water, cause it thus to happen, that on seeing her pitcher the water shall vanish, and again slowly re-appear. In this way she will be delayed. May the water not flow into her pitcher, and you keep the maiden as your own." At noon when she went to bring water, it suddenly dried up before her, and she began to weep. Then after a while the water began slowly to rise. When it reached her ankles she tried to fill her pitcher, but it would not go under the water. Being frightened she began to wail as follows;—

---

[1] The spirit believed to preside over a certain class of rice land.

> *"Oh! my brother, the water reaches to my ankles,*
> *Oh! my brother, the water reaches to my ankles,*
> *Still, Oh! my brother, the pitcher will not dip,*
> *Still, Oh! my brother, the pitcher will not dip."*

The water continued to rise until it reached her knee, when she began to wail as follows;—

> *"Oh! my brother, the water reaches to my knee,*
> *Oh! my brother, the water reaches to my knee,*
> *Still, Oh! my brother, the pitcher will not dip,*
> *Still, Oh! my brother, the pitcher will not dip."*

The water continued to rise, and when it reached her waist, she wailed as follows;—

> *"Oh! my brother, the water reaches to my waist,*
> *"Oh! my brother, the water reaches to my waist,*
> *"Still, Oh! my brother, the pitcher will not dip,*
> *"Still, Oh! my brother, the pitcher will not dip."*

The water in the tank continued to rise, and when it reached her breast, she wailed as follows;—

> *"Oh! my brother, the water reaches to my breast,*
> *"Oh! my brother, the water reaches to my breast,*
> *"Still, Oh! my brother, the pitcher will not fill,*
> *"Still, Oh! my brother, the pitcher will not fill."*

The water still rose, and when it reached her neck she wailed as follows;—

> *"Oh! my brother, the water reaches to my neck,*

"Oh! my brother, the water reaches to my neck,
"Still, Oh! my brother, the pitcher will not dip,
"Still, Oh! my brother, the pitcher will not dip."

At length the water became so deep that she felt herself to be drowning, then she wailed as follows;—

"Oh! my brother, the water measures a man's height,
"Oh! my brother, the water measures a man's height,
"Oh! my brother, the pitcher begins to fill,
"Oh! my brother, the pitcher begins to fill."

The pitcher filled with water, and along with it she sank and was drowned. The bonga then transformed her into a bonga like himself, and carried her off.

After a time she re-appeared as a bamboo growing on the embankment of the tank in which she had been drowned. When the bamboo had grown to an immense size, a Jugi, who was in the habit of passing that way, seeing it, said to himself, this will make a splendid fiddle. So one day he brought an axe to cut it down; but when he was about to begin, the bamboo exclaimed, "Do not cut at the root, cut higher up." When he lifted his axe to cut high up the stem, the bamboo cried out, "Do not cut near the top, cut at the root." When the Jugi again prepared himself to cut at the root as requested, the bamboo said, "Do not cut at the root, cut higher up;" and when he was about to cut higher up, it again called out to him, "Do not cut high up, cut at the root." The Jugi by this time was aware that a bonga was trying to frighten him, so becoming angry he cut down the bamboo at the root, and taking it away made a fiddle out of it. The instrument had a superior tone and delighted all who heard it. The Jugi carried it with him when he went a-begging, and through the influence of its sweet music he returned home every evening with a full wallet.

He now and again visited, when on his rounds, the house of the bonga girl's brothers, and the strains of the fiddle affected them greatly. Some of them were moved even to tears, for the fiddle seemed to wail as one in bitter anguish. The elder brother wished to purchase it, and offered to support the Jugi for a whole year, if he would consent to part with his magical instrument. The Jugi, however, knew its value, and refused to sell it.

It so happened that the Jugi sometime after went to the house of a village chief, and after playing a tune or two on his fiddle asked something to eat. They offered to buy his fiddle and promised a high price for it, but he rejected all such overtures, his fiddle being to him his means of livelihood. When they saw that he was not to be prevailed upon, they gave him food and a plentiful supply of liquor. Of the latter he partook so freely that he presently became intoxicated. While he was in this condition, they took away his fiddle, and substituted their own old one for it. When the Jugi recovered, he missed his instrument, and suspecting that it had been stolen requested them to return it to him. They denied having taken it, so he had to depart, leaving his fiddle behind him. The chief's son being a musician, used to play on the Jugi's fiddle, and in his hands the music it gave forth delighted the ears of all within hearing.

When all the household were absent at their labours in the fields, the bonga girl emerged from the bamboo fiddle, and prepared the family meal. Having partaken of her own share, she placed that of the chiefs son under his bed, and covering it up to keep off the dust, re-entered the fiddle. This happening every day the other members of the household were under the impression that some female neighbour of theirs was in this manner showing her interest in the young man, so they did not trouble themselves to find out how it came about. The young chief, however, was determined to watch, and see which of his lady friends was so attentive to his comfort. He said in his own mind, "I will catch her to-day, and give her a sound beating. She is causing me to be ashamed before the others." So saying, he hid himself in a corner in a pile of firewood. In a short time the girl came out of the bamboo fiddle, and began to dress her hair. Having completed her toilet, she cooked the meal of rice as usual, and having partaken herself, she placed the young man's portion under his bed, as she was wont, and was about to enter the fiddle again, when he running out from his hiding place caught her in his arms. The bonga girl exclaimed, "Fie! Fie! you may be a Dom,[2] or you may be a Hadi."[2] He said, "No. But from to-day, you and I are one." So they began lovingly to hold converse with each other. When the others returned home in the evening, they saw that she was both a human being and a bonga, and they rejoiced exceedingly.

Through course of time the bonga girl's family became very poor, and her brothers on one occasion came to the chief's house on a visit.

The bonga girl recognised them at once, but they did not know who she was. She brought them water on their arrival, and afterwards set cooked rice before them. Then sitting down near them, she began in wailing tones to upbraid them on account of the treatment she had been subjected to by their wives. She related all that had befallen her, and wound up by saying, "It is probable that you knew it all, and yet you did not interfere to save me."

After a time she became reconciled to her sisters-in-law, and no longer harboured enmity in her mind against them, for the injury they had done her.

---

[2] Semi-Hinduised aborigines, whose touch is considered polluting.

Gumda the Hero

There was once a certain fatherless lad named Gumda. His occupation was to tend the raja's goats. He, and his mother lived in a small house at the end of the street in which the raja's palace was situated. The raja's mahout was in the habit of taking his elephant along that street, and every time it passed, it rubbed itself against the wall of Gumda's house. One day at noon it so happened that Gumda was at home when the elephant was being taken to the tank to drink, and as usual he rubbed his side against the house as he passed. Gumda was incensed with the elephant for thus destroying his house, and coming out quickly, said to the mahout, "What although it is the raja's elephant! I could take hold of any person's elephant by the trunk, and throw it across seven seas." The elephant understood what Gumda had said, and he refused to go down into the water, and would not even drink. On being brought home he would not eat his grain, nor would he so much as look at water. He continued thus so long that he began to grow lean and weak. The mahout knew that it was Gumda's curse that had so affected his charge. The raja one day noticing the altered condition of his elephant, said to the mahout, "Why has the elephant become so emaciated?" The mahout replied, "Oh! raja, one day at noon Gumda abused him. He said, 'If you were not the raja's elephant,

I would take you by the trunk and throw you across seven seas.' 'Every day,' he said, 'he rubs himself against my house.' Since then the elephant has refused his food and water." The raja, on hearing this, commanded that Gumda be brought before him. The messenger found him at home, and brought him into the presence of the raja who asked him, "Is it true, Gumda, that you said you would throw the elephant as you would a stone?" Gumda replied, "Yes, it is quite true that I said so. The elephant every time it passes along the street rubs itself against the wall of my house, and being angry, I said these words. Now, do with me whatsoever you please." The raja marvelled greatly on hearing Gumda's reply, and addressing him said, "Now my lad, prove your words, for prove them you must. If you succeed in thus throwing an elephant, I shall present you with a large estate." The raja appointed the tenth day following as that on which Gumda should wrestle with the elephant; and he, after receiving permission from the raja, returned home.

The raja in the interval caused proclamation to be made to all his subjects, ordering them to be present on the day when Gumda was to meet the elephant in mortal combat. On the morning of the appointed day Gumda was found baking bread. As he did not appear punctually in the arena, the raja sent a messenger to bring him. On arriving at Gumda's house, he found him baking bread. He said to him, "Come along, the raja has asked for you." Gumda said, "Wait a little till I partake of some refreshment." He invited the messenger to be seated, and he also sat down as if to eat, but instead of eating the bread, he began to throw it at the man, and continued doing so until he had buried him under eight maunds of loaves. The poor fellow cried out, "Oh Gumda, come and release me, of a truth I am almost crushed to death under this heap of bread." He removed the bread from above him, and he immediately returned to the raja. As he was leaving the house he saw 12 maunds of cooked rice, evidently intended for Gumda's dinner. Coming into the presence of the raja he said, "Oh! raja, I saw in Gumda's house twelve maunds of cooked rice, and he threw a loaf of bread weighing eight maunds at me, which almost crushed me to death. It is quite possible that he may win."

At length Gumda came bringing with him a sledge hammer weighing twelve maunds, and a shield of the same weight. The contest was to take place on a plain sufficiently large to accommodate an immense number of spectators.

Then the fight began. The two combatants attacked each other so furiously that they raised such a cloud of dust as to completely conceal them from the onlookers. The elephant could not long sustain the unequal combat, and when he was beaten, Gumda seized him by the trunk, and threw him over the seas. Owing to the darkness caused by the clouds of dust, none of the thousands present noticed the elephant as he went, flying over their heads high up in the air.

When the dust subsided, Gumda was found sitting alone, the elephant was nowhere to be seen. The raja called the victor to him, and said, "What have you done with the elephant?" Gumda replied "I flung him early in the forenoon over seven seas." Hearing his answer and not seeing the elephant, they all marvelled greatly.

The raja then said to Gumda, "Well, you have thrown the elephant somewhere. You must now go in search of its bones." Gumda went home and said to his mother, "Make up a parcel of food for me, I am going to find the elephant's bones." She complied with his request and he set out.

As he hurried along intent upon his quest, he found a man fishing with a Palmyra palm tree as a rod, and a full grown elephant as a bait. On seeing him Gumda exclaimed, "You are indeed a great hero." The man replied, "I am no hero, the widow's son Gumda is the great hero, for did not he fling the raja's elephant across seven seas?" Gumda said, "I am he." The fisherman said," I will go with you." Gumda replied, "Come along!"

As Gumda and his attendant went on their way, they came to a field in which a number of men were hoeing, and their master, to shield them from the heat of the sun, stood holding over them, as an umbrella, a large Pepul tree.[1] Gumda seeing him said, "You are a hero and no mistake." The man replied, "No indeed, I am no hero. Gumda, the widow's son, threw the raja's elephant across seven seas. He is the hero." Gumda said, "I am he." "Then," said the man, "I also will go with you." "Follow me," said Gumda, and the three proceeded on their way.

As they journeyed they fell in with two men, who were raising water from a tank for irrigating purposes by merely singing. When Gumda saw them, he exclaimed, "You two are heroes indeed." They answered, "What do you see heroic in us? There is one hero, Gumda by name, he threw a raja's elephant across seven seas." Gumda said, "I am he." The men exclaimed, "We also will follow you." Gumda said, "Follow." And the five men went forth to search for the elephant's bones.

On and on they went until they reached the sea, which they crossed, and entered the primeval forest beyond. Selecting a suitable place they encamped, and began the search for the elephant's bones. The first day the fisherman was left in the camp to cook the food,

---

[1] Ficus religiosa, Willd. one of the hugest of India's many huge trees.

while the others went out into the forest. Near by a certain jugi raja resided in a cave in a rock. He came to the camp just as the food was cooked, and said to the fisherman, "Give me some rice to eat." He declined, and the jugi raja then said, "Will you give me rice, or will you fight with me?" He replied, "I have prepared this food with difficulty and prefer fighting to giving it up." So they fought, and the jugi raja was victor. He laid a heavy stone on the breast of the cook, and then devoured all the food. There had been twelve maunds of rice prepared, and he left none. After a long time he released his victim, and then went his way. Being released the fisherman set about preparing more food, but before it was ready, his companions returned and seeing the pot still on the fire, they enquired why he had not made haste with his cooking. He replied, "I have not been idle, I have spent all the time in cooking." He did not tell them about the jugi raja having been at the camp.

The next day another of the company remained as cook, while the others went out to search in the forest for the elephant's bones. The jugi raja again visited the camp, and the scene of the previous day was re-enacted. But he also did not speak of the visit of the jugi raja to the others when they returned. In this way the jugi raja encountered each in turn till only Gumda was left, and he remained in the camp to cook. When he had got the rice cooked, the jugi raja made his appearance and said, "Will you fight with me, or will you give up the food?" Gumda replied, "I will not give you the food. I have spent much time in cooking it, and when those who have gone in search of the elephant's bones return, what shall I set before them, if I give it to you now? You have played this trick every day, and have put my companions to much trouble, but to-day we have met." So they fought. Gumda overpowered the jugi raja, and killed him with the stone he used to put upon the breast of those whom he vanquished. He then espoused the jugi raja's wife, and took possession of his kingdom. Gumda's companions held him in great awe, because each in turn had been conquered by the jugi raja, but Gumda had experienced little difficulty in putting him to death.

Gumda became raja of that country, and when he had settled his affairs, he sent for his mother to come and reside with him. The raja, whom Gumda had previously served, sought his friendship, and withdrew his command to Gumda to search for the elephant's bones until he found them. The prowess of Gumda caused him to deprecate his anger. He said, "If I offend him, he will kill me as he did the jugi raja, and take my wife and kingdom, as he did his."

Lipi and Lapra

Once upon a time there were seven brothers. At first they were very poor, but afterwards they became comparatively rich, and were in position to lay out a little money at usury. The affairs of the youngest prospered most, so that before long he became the wealthiest of them all.

Each of the seven brothers planted fruit trees, and every day after they returned from their work, before they sat down to meat, they watered them. In process of time all the trees flowered, but the flowers on the eldest brother's trees withered and dropped off the day they appeared. The trees of the other brothers failed to ripen their fruit, but those of the youngest brother were laden with delicious fruit which ripened to perfection. Five of the brothers said to him, "You are very fortunate in having such a splendid crop;" but the eldest brother was envious of his good fortune, and resolved to be revenged upon him.

The youngest brother brought up two puppies, whom he named Lipi and Lapra. They turned out good hunting dogs, and by their aid their master used to keep the family larder well supplied. The others were pleased to see so much game brought to the house.

One day they said to him, "Take us also to where you get your large game." To this he agreed, and they accompanied him to his usual hunting ground. Game was plentiful, but they could kill nothing, although every time he shot an arrow he brought down his animal. Five of his brothers praised him for his skill, and accuracy of aim, but the eldest brother, not having succeeded in bagging anything himself, envied him still more, and was confirmed in his desire for revenge.

It so happened that one day all the brothers, with the exception of the eldest and the youngest, went out to their work. The eldest brother finding himself alone with his youngest brother proposed that they should go together to the hill for the purpose of procuring fibre to make ropes. He said, "Come let us go to the hill to cut lar."[1] His brother replied, "Come, let us set out." He, however, wished to take his dogs with him, but his brother said, "Why should you tire them by taking them so far? Leave them behind." But he replied, "I shall not go, unless you allow me to take them with me. How shall we be able to bring home venison if they do not accompany us? They may kill some game on the way." As he insisted, he was permitted to do as he desired, and they set out for the hill.

As they went on their way they came to a spring, and the elder said, "Tie up the two dogs here. I know all this forest, and there is no game to be found in it." The younger was averse to leaving his dogs behind him, but as his brother seemed determined he should do so, he tied them with a stout rope to a tree. His brother said, "See that you make them secure, so that they may not break loose and run away, and be lost."

---

[1] The fibre yielded by Bauhinia Vahlii, W. and A. goes under that name among the Santals.

A low hill lay between them, and the high one on which the trees grew which yielded the lar. This they surmounted, and descending into the valley that divided them began the ascent, and soon reached the place where their work was to be. They soon cut and peeled sufficient lar, and sitting down twisted it into strong ropes. Just as they had prepared to return home, the elder brother seized the younger, and bound him with the ropes they had made. He then grasped his sickle with the intention of putting him to death. The helpless young man thought of his dogs, and in a loud voice wailed as follows;—

> *Come, come, Lipi and Lapra,*
> *Cross the low hill*
> *On to the slope of the high.*

He called them again and again. The dogs heard the voice, and struggled to get loose, and at length, by a great effort, they succeeded in breaking the ropes with which they were bound, and ran in the direction from which the sound proceeded. Now and again the cries ceased, and they stood still until they again heard them, when they ran as before. Having reached the valley that separated the two hills, they could no longer hear the wailing as before, and they were greatly perplexed. They ran hither and thither, hoping to catch it again, but not doing so they directed their course to the large hill, on reaching the foot of which it again became audible. They now recognized the voice of their master, and ran rapidly forward.

When the elder brother saw the dogs approaching, he quickly aimed a blow with the sickle at his younger brother's head, but he, jerking aside, escaped. Before there was time for him to strike again, the dogs had arrived, and their master hounded them upon his assailant and they quickly tore him to pieces. They then bit through the ropes with which his brother had bound him, and set him at liberty. He then returned home accompanied by his dogs, and when they enquired of him where his brother was, he replied, "He left me to follow a deer, I cannot say what direction he took. We did not meet again." He wept as he related this, and they enquired, "Why do you weep?" He said, "My two dogs lay down on the ground, and howled, and fear possesses me that some wild beast has devoured my brother."

The next day a party went in search of him, and found him as the dogs had left him. When they saw him lying torn and bloody, they said, "Some wild beast has done this."

They brought the body home, and committed it to the flames of the funeral pile, and sorrowfully performed all the ceremonies usual on such occasions.

After the death of the elder brother, they all lived together in peace and harmony.